D0045271

GHOST DETECTORS
Monsters!

BOOK 12

BY
DOTTI ENDERLE

ILLUSTRATED BY
HOWARD MCWILLIAM

magic
wagon

visit us at www.abdopublishing.com

A big thank you to Adrienne Enderle — DE
With thanks to my ever-supportive wife Rebecca — HM

Published by Magic Wagon, a division of the ABDO Group,
8000 West 78th Street, Edina, Minnesota 55439. Copyright
© 2012 by Abdo Consulting Group, Inc. International copyrights
reserved in all countries. All rights reserved. No part of this
book may be reproduced in any form without written permission
from the publisher.

Calico Chapter Books™ is a trademark and logo of Magic Wagon.

Printed in the United States of America
052011
092011
♻ This book contains at least 10% recycled materials.

Text by Dotti Enderle
Illustrations by Howard McWilliam
Edited by Stephanie Hedlund and Rochelle Baltzer
Cover and interior design by Jaime Martens

Library of Congress Cataloging-in-Publication Data

Enderle, Dotti, 1954-
  Monsters! / by Dotti Enderle ; illustrated by Howard McWilliam.
     p. cm. -- (Ghost Detectors ; bk. 12)
  ISBN 978-1-61641-628-7
  [1. Monsters--Fiction. 2. Ghosts--Fiction. 3. Motion picture
theaters--Fiction. 4. Humorous stories.] I. McWilliam, Howard,
1977- ill. II. Title.
  PZ7.E69645Mo 2011
  [Fic]--dc22
                              2011001845

Contents

Face-Friends?

Malcolm opened one eye, then the next. Hmmm . . . It was awfully quiet for a Saturday morning. He sat up, yawned, and scratched his moppy bedhead. *Where is everybody?*

It was obvious that his sister, Cocoa, was gone—no size-ten, clomping feet or teeth-grinding, whiny twang.

His stomach growled like a monster. Must. Eat. He crawled out of bed in search of food. Surely Mom had whipped

up a wonderfully tasty breakfast of . . .
Huh? The kitchen was empty and clean.
No eggs. No oatmeal. No waffles.

Malcolm poured a bowl of Fancy Flakes,
drowned them in milk, and shoveled them
in. After the last floating flake had been
swallowed, he gulped the milk right out
of the bowl.

He rinsed his dishes, then wandered
through the house looking for signs of life.
Just when he thought he was all alone, he
found Grandma Eunice sitting at his dad's
computer. Her eyes were narrowed in
concentration, and her tongue poked out
of the corner of her mouth as she typed.

"Where's Mom?" Malcolm asked.

Grandma Eunice didn't look up.
"Cocoa joined the debate club, and your
mother volunteered to chaperone today's
tournament."

Malcolm scratched his head. "Cocoa's on the debate team?"

"Yep," Grandma answered. "Go figure."

Malcolm couldn't imagine Cocoa ever winning a debate without screaming, "Just shut up!"

"Can you do me a favor?" Malcolm asked.

Grandma still kept her eyes straight on the computer. "Not right now, I'm busy."

"Just a small favor," he egged.

"I'm almost done," she said, *peck, peck, pecking* at the keyboard.

He hated asking but, "I need to borrow some money."

Grandma Eunice didn't even look up. She still pecked away at the computer.

"Grandma, what are you doing?"

"I'm trying to set up a Face-Friends page," she answered.

What? Why would Grandma want a Face-Friends page? Did she even have any friends?

Malcolm watched her *tip-tap* at the keyboard. She tilted her head this way and that. Once in a while she'd lean really close, examining what she'd typed.

This could take forever, he thought. "Uh, do you need some help?" he asked.

"Nope. I've got it." She fiddled some more, filling in the boxes on the page. "Hmmm . . . Do you think I should lie about my age?"

Malcolm shrugged. "Might as well. No one would believe your real age anyway."

"Hey!" Grandma fussed. "I'm not that old."

"There are fossils younger than you, Grandma," Malcolm teased.

"Maybe. But can a fossil do this?" Grandma backed up her wheelchair, stood up, and did a little jig. Then she plopped back down and wheeled back to the computer. "Yep. I think I'll shave twenty years off my age. It'll be our little secret."

"Yeah, our secret," Malcolm said with a sly grin. "I won't tell . . . as long as you loan me some money."

Grandma Eunice winked. "There's no doubt about it. You definitely take after my side of the family. What'd you need the money for?"

"The old Bijou movie theater is closing down," Malcolm said. "So they've been running old classic films. This weekend

they're showing monster movies. Dandy and I are going to spend the whole day there."

"Ah, the old Bijou Theater," Grandma reminisced. "My boyfriend took me there to see *Gone with the Wind*."

Ew. Malcolm didn't want to think about Grandma having a boyfriend. "So will you loan me some money?"

"Will you be my Face-Friend?" Grandma asked.

"I don't have a Face-Friends page," Malcolm admitted. He didn't particularly want one either.

Grandma sighed. "Fine. Get some money out of my purse."

"Thanks, Grandma!" Malcolm cheered as he hurried off to meet Dandy.

Horrorfest!

Malcolm and Dandy straddled their bikes as they looked up at the Bijou marquee.

SATURDAY & SUNDAY
HORRORFEST!
Featuring all your movie monster favorites.
*Frankenstein, The Wolfman, Dracula, Godzilla,
The Mummy & The Creature from the Black Lagoon*
Don't miss one horrific moment!

"This is going to be awesome!" Malcolm said. "I hope they show them in the same

order as the sign. I want to see *Frankenstein* first."

"Yeah," Dandy agreed. "Then *The Wolfman. Woo-oo-oo!*" he howled. "Then *Godzilla,* then—" His face pickled into a sour frown.

Malcolm knew exactly what Dandy was thinking. "Maybe we should skip *The Mummy,*" he said, remembering their recent encounter with the ghost of the mummified Pharaoh Tuturtikum.

They locked up their bikes and walked over to the ticket booth.

The girl inside the glass booth was popping bubblegum and reading a magazine.

"One ticket please," Dandy said, pushing a dollar toward her. It was then that the girl decided to blow a bubble.

The gum inflated like a balloon—bigger and bigger and bigger.

This can't be good, Malcolm thought as Dandy stepped back.

The bubble was now the size of a basketball. It grew so big, it actually picked up Dandy's dollar off the counter.

They both watched as the bubble continued to expand, Dandy's dollar pushing back toward him. He reached for it when – *Snap!* – the gum popped, covering the girl's chin. Dandy's dollar was stuck to her neck.

"I hate it when that happens," she said, picking off a few of the stringy strands. Then she looked back at Dandy. "That'll be one dollar."

"I gave you a dollar," he told her, pointing to her neck.

She didn't seem to notice. Instead she searched the counter and the floor. With squinted eyes, she looked back at Dandy. "That'll be one dollar."

"I gave you a dollar."

He reached over to pluck the bill from her neck but— "Stop it!" she squealed, swatting Dandy with the rolled-up magazine. "I'll call the cops!"

"The dollar is stuck to your neck!" Malcolm yelled, pulling Dandy away.

The girl reached up, peeled it off, then handed Dandy his ticket. "Next!" she called.

Malcolm looked behind him. He was the only one left in line. He placed the dollar on the counter and snatched up his ticket. Then he and Dandy rushed inside.

The boys weighed themselves down with a jumbo popcorn, jelly beans, two Choco-Loco bars, and two root beers. Then Malcolm said, "Let's sit in the balcony!"

They followed the faded carpet up the stairs, trudged across the sticky balcony floor, then plopped down on the first row.

"How high up are we?" Dandy asked. They both leaned over the rail, spilling a few kernels of popcorn. They drifted down and landed on a woman with hair like whipped cream.

"It's kind of a long drop," Dandy said. "I'm getting sort of dizzy."

"Then let's just watch the movie," Malcolm said, sitting back.

Malcolm figured the Bijou had once been ritzy and regal with velvety drapes and sparkling chandeliers. Now it was

faded and cracked and smelled like the inside of an old sleeping bag.

Soon the dusty green curtains opened and the theater went dark. Malcolm slouched down in his seat as *Frankenstein* rolled onto the screen.

Three black-and-white movies later, Malcolm and Dandy walked out into the world of color.

"That was awesome!" Malcolm said. "We're definitely coming back tomorrow."

Dandy quietly unlocked his bike. His face looked like a giant green jelly bean. "Maybe we shouldn't have had so much butter on the popcorn."

"Are you going to be all right?"

Dandy placed his hand on his stomach, opened his mouth wide, and – *buuuurrrp!* "I'll be fine."

Malcolm looked toward the west where the sun was just a glazed donut dunking fast. "We better get back before dark."

They took off, pedaling away from traffic. Malcolm's head was still filled with Hollywood horror. He hadn't had this much fun since Halloween. But when they turned off the main road, Dandy hit the brakes.

"Did you see that?" Dandy asked, tilting toward a storm drain.

Malcolm only saw the large, rectangular opening. "See what?"

"Eyes. I just saw a huge pair of goggle eyes looking out at us."

"It's just your imagination."

Dandy leaned closer to the drain. "I didn't imagine it."

"Dandy, you just sat through three monster movies. You're seeing things. Let's go."

"But what if it's an animal trapped down there?" Dandy said. "Shouldn't we try to rescue it?"

If it was a trapped animal, Malcolm felt bad for it, but he said, "It's too dangerous. We need to get going. It's getting dark."

"There!" Dandy said, pointing.

Malcolm looked again and now there were two huge, lidless eyes staring right at them. "What is that?"

It didn't take long to find out. The thing inside the drain pushed one scaly arm out, then the other. It pulled itself up, poking its fish-like head out, gills and all. When it finally made its way out, the large reptile-man towered over them.

"Oh no!" Malcolm shouted. "Go! Go!"

They both shot off, pedaling for their lives. Three blocks later they slowed down a bit. Malcolm's heart raced, and Dandy was hyperventilating.

"Was that . . . was that . . . was that?" Dandy stuttered between breaths.

"Yes!" Malcolm said. "It was the Creature from the Black Lagoon!"

Video Invasion

"It was just our imaginations," Malcolm decided as he and Dandy sat in his basement lab the next day.

"It was real!" Dandy insisted. "We both saw the same thing."

Malcolm shook his head. "It couldn't have been the Creature from the Black Lagoon. That's impossible."

"It was him," Dandy said. "Gills, eyes, scales . . . he was even dripping."

"That's what I mean," Malcolm said. "It hasn't rained in days. That storm drain was dry. It couldn't have been him."

They both gave up arguing and sat quietly. Finally Malcolm said, "Do you want to go back for the rest of Horrorfest today?" He could tell by the freaked-out look on Dandy's face that the answer was no. That was fine with Malcolm. He'd had his fill of monsters yesterday.

"Let's play a video game," he said, loading Alien Paintball into the game box. Sure he could've chosen Road Rangers or Battle Snakes or Star Grazers, but Alien Paintball posed more of a challenge. And of all Malcolm's video games it was definitely the most colorful!

Dandy chose his alien for the battle.

"You always pick that one," Malcolm complained.

"It's my favorite," Dandy said, thumbing the game controller. Dandy always picked the alien called Slovart. It looked like a cross between an armadillo and a giraffe. "The paintballs bounce off his armor."

"But his neck is longer than a fire ladder. That's what I always aim for," Malcolm pointed out.

"Slovart has more paint barrels than the others," Dandy said. True. Slovart's head had four ears, three noses, fifteen fingers, and a corkscrew tail that shot paintballs on command.

Then Malcolm selected his alien. Brackensphere—an alien that had burst through the stratosphere with one mission and one mission only: to tag all other Earth-invading aliens with gobbledygook. And Malcolm liked that Brackensphere had a

spout on his belly button that released a long spray of neon orange.

Once the aliens were selected and the paint loaded, the battle was on. Malcolm thumbed the control, dodging paintballs and firing missile globs at Dandy's alien. But Dandy fired back, layering Malcolm's extraterrestrial with a series of shots that looked like a four-layer ice-cream cone.

"Hey!" Malcolm said. "You're winning."

Dandy held tight to the controller, swaying back and forth as he dodged, ducked, and spewed paint. "I know! I never win."

Malcolm tried making a comeback, but Dandy was too quick.

"*Ha, ha, ha.* I'm beating you," Dandy teased. He twisted Slovart's neck around Brackensphere's wings, and – *Pow! Pow! Pow!* – earned an extra ten points.

Brackensphere made a dive for Slovart and was about to release a bucketful of blueberry goo when a strange, dinosaurlike creature appeared on the screen.

"What are you doing, Dandy?" Malcolm asked, swerving his creature away.

"It's not me," Dandy answered.

The creature stomped closer and closer. Malcolm leaned in close. "What is that? He's not one of the aliens in the game."

"Maybe it's an upgrade," Dandy suggested. "He got added somehow."

"How?" Malcolm asked. "This game isn't linked to anything online."

Dandy still thumbed his controller, trying to keep Slovart away from the new invader. "He's gotta be a part of the game."

"But he doesn't even look like an alien," Malcolm said.

That's when the creature's scales glowed electric blue. "*Ayerrrrrrr*," he roared, blasting atomic fire from his mouth.

"Malcolm . . .," Dandy said, frozen in place.

"I know," Malcolm finished, "it's not an alien. It's . . ."

"Godzilla!" they both shouted at the same time.

Dandy's hands quivered. "How did he get into the game?"

Malcolm was speechless. He had no clue.

"What should we do?" Dandy asked.

"Let's blast him!"

They turned their aliens and fired. Paintball after paintball soared toward him. Red. Green. Purple. Yellow. Godzilla just batted them away. *Ayerrrrrrr!*

Malcolm tapped the controller button with sonic speed. But when the paint hit Godzilla, it melted away into colorful goo.

Then something even more amazing happened. All the other paintball aliens rose up.

Malcolm and Dandy froze.

"How is that possible?" Malcolm said. "We only selected two players."

Dandy just sat, mouth gaping. "Maybe we're dreaming."

"What?" Malcolm said.

"Sometimes after I play this game, I have nightmares about the aliens swapping my toothpaste for a tube of moss-green finger paint."

"We're not dreaming, Dandy."

"Are you sure?" Dandy asked. He blinked several times, testing it out.

Malcolm reached over and pinched Dandy's arm.

"Ouch!"

"See?" Malcolm said. "We're not dreaming."

"I'm not, but what about you?" Dandy asked, pinching Malcolm's ear.

"Stop it!" Malcolm said, swatting Dandy's hand away.

"I was just checking," Dandy said. "It could've been your nightmare."

"I think it's a waking nightmare," Malcolm said, pointing to the video screen.

Godzilla wreaked havoc on the alien city. He trampled trees, buildings, satellites, and radars. *Ayerrrrrrr!*

"I don't believe this," Malcolm said. "He's crushing all our creatures."

"What do you think we should do?" Dandy asked.

Godzilla stomped closer to the screen. *Ayerrrrrrr!* More blue radiation shot from his mouth.

Malcolm didn't know what to do. "He's coming right at us," he said, scootching back. "The characters never get this close."

With every clomp, the video monitor shook. Godzilla grew closer . . . and closer . . . and closer!

Malcolm flipped the power button. The machine didn't turn off. But Godzilla stomped closer . . . and closer . . .

Ayerrrrrrr! When his scaly face filled the screen, he breathed electric blue beams of fire straight at the boys.

"Ahhhh!" Dandy screamed as he ducked behind Malcolm.

The video screen emitted a blinding flash, then bubbled like a film reel that'd gotten too close to a hot bulb. Everything went dark.

"What just happened?" Dandy asked.

Malcolm was too stunned to answer. He tried sorting the mystery in his head, but his thoughts were as speckled as the paint splatters.

"This is crazy. How did Godzilla get into the video game?"

Dandy shrugged. "Maybe it was a crossover."

"A crossover?"

"Yeah. Maybe two video games got mixed up." Dandy suggested.

"I don't think that's possible," Malcolm said. "And if it were, what other video

game do I own that features Japanese monsters?"

Dandy nodded. "I see what you mean. Even if there is a game like that, I wouldn't buy it."

"No kidding," Malcolm said. "Who wants a game that you can't control?"

They turned and looked at each other, eyes wide. Malcolm hopped over to the game box and pulled out the disc. It was heat warped, smoky, and still hot.

"Here's the problem," Malcolm said, flipping the disc back and forth

for inspection. "I think it must've been an electrical problem. Oh well, I was kinda tired of playing this game anyway."

"Yeah," Dandy agreed. "And I was tired of dreaming about finger paint toothpaste, too."

Just as Malcolm tossed the damaged disc into the trash, the video screen shook. Within the darkness they heard, *Ayerrrrrrr!*

They both shot up the stairs and out of the basement, slamming the door shut.

"Did we just imagine that, too?" Dandy asked.

Wall Worry

Malcolm just couldn't understand it. How had Godzilla and the Creature from the Black Lagoon wormed their way out of their films? It was crazy . . . nuts . . . absolutely bonkers! It just couldn't be real. Or could it?

At school the next day, every little noise startled Malcolm out of his seat. The whirring of the pencil sharpener sounded like a swarm of killer bees. The *scritch-scratching* of pencils was like hungry rats,

clawing through the walls. And Mrs. Dupont, the crabby old lunch lady, looked and sounded like Frankenstein's monster . . . *Grrrrr!* He just couldn't escape it.

Malcolm finally made it home, ready to relax and enjoy dinner. But when he stepped into the kitchen . . .

"My life is ruined!"

Only his sister, Cocoa, could blast a squeal so piercing it made his teeth hurt.

His mom, who was slicing a roast, sighed. "What now, Cocoa?"

Cocoa stood sobbing in her electric purple dress with pink fishnet stockings. She held up her laptop.

"Look what's she's done!" Cocoa shouted. "Grandma Eunice posted this on my Face-Friends page!" She was crying

so hard her mascara ran in little spikes down her cheeks.

Malcolm leaned over so he could read it. In big letters it said:

Hey, Cocoa, it's your grandma typing this. You left your undies hanging on the shower rod again. I accidentally knocked them off when I took a bath. Not all of them got wet, but the ones with the teeny red hearts are soaked. Love, Grandma Eunice.

"Mom! All my friends saw this! I'll never be able to face them again!"

Everyone turned to look at Grandma Eunice, who had rolled up to the table and was buttering a roll.

"I don't know what all the fuss is about," she said. "I put the undies in the dryer."

Malcolm could tell that his mom was around Level Three on the countdown to a major headache.

"You could've just told Cocoa," Mom said calmly. "You didn't have to announce it to all her friends."

Grandma slapped on another layer of butter. "It wasn't just her friends. My friends saw it, too."

Malcolm couldn't believe it. "Grandma, you just signed on yesterday. How many friends do you have?"

"Over 700 now."

Everyone stood paralyzed for a moment.

"Seven hundred?" Mom said.

"Seven hundred!" Cocoa screeched, causing Malcolm's teeth to tingle again.

Malcolm was just too curious. "How did you get 700 friends in twenty-four hours?"

Grandma ripped a bite of her roll. "I had a method."

They all waited. Mom tapped her foot.

"Okay," she gave in. "I sent out an e-mail to Face-Friends Fogies. It's a network of old people who've actually figured out how to use a computer."

"And you got 700 friends that fast?" Malcolm said.

Grandma ripped another bite of roll. "Yeah. Who knew there were 700 old folks who can use a computer?"

Zzzzzzz!

***

Malcolm's teacher, Mrs. Goolsby, had laid the homework on thick. Ugh! He didn't have time to think about movies or monsters or beastly lunch ladies. By the time he closed his math book, his eyes were closing, too.

He crawled into bed with just the neon glow of his alarm clock lighting the room. Everyone was asleep and the house was quiet, except for the mammoth snores of Grandma Eunice. *Snort-snort-snort-snort-snort.*

Malcolm was about to drift off to dreamland when he heard, *zzzz . . . zzzz . . . zzzz . . . zzzz.* He sat up straight as a pencil. *What was that?* Holding his breath, he waited. The glow of the clock cast some creepy shadows on the wall. He listened close. *Snort-snort-snort-snort-snort.* Ah . . . just Grandma Eunice again.

He scrunched back down in the bed, pulling the covers up to his chin. He tried to relax, but . . . Did that shadow on the closet move? It stretched long and thin, with fingerlike branches touching the knob.

Ridiculous, he thought. *It's* the same shadow he saw night after night. But a shadow of what? He had never stopped to worry about that before.

Malcolm sat up again, scanning the room for the source. *I really need to pick up*

in here, he thought, looking at the clutter. Then he spotted it. *Phew!* It was just his Star-Master Cyborg action figure invading his science fair trophy on his dresser.

Calm down, he told himself. When he lay back down this time, he pulled the pillow over his head. *Now,* he thought. He let out a long deep breath and closed his eyes. The house was still silent, well,

except for *snort-snort-snort-snort-snort*. He was fine with that. But it lasted only a minute or so.

Zzzz . . . zzzz . . . zzzz . . . zzzz.

Malcolm shot up again. "What's making that noise?" he asked out loud.

Zzzz . . . zzzz . . . zzzz . . . zzzz.

Malcolm sat, frozen. It was louder that time.

Zzzz . . . zzzz . . . zzzz . . . zzzz.

The green glow of the clock had a Frankenstein feel to it, giving him goose bumps. He listened closely.

Zzzz . . . zzzz . . . zzzz . . . zzzz.

It was coming from beneath the bed.

Zzzz . . . zzzz . . . zzzz . . . zzzz.

Maybe he should turn on a light?

Zzzz . . . zzzz . . . zzzz . . . zzzz.

But that would mean getting out of bed . . .

Zzzz . . . zzzz . . . zzzz . . . zzzz.

. . . putting his feet on the floor . . .

Zzzz . . . zzzz . . . zzzz . . . zzzz.

Wait! He could jump to the door and run out.

Zzzz . . . zzzz . . . zzzz . . . zzzz.

The noise grew louder. It sounded like someone, or something, drilling up through his mattress. Could it burrow its way to the top, grab him, and pull him down into the darkness, never to be seen again?

Zzzz . . . zzzz . . . zzzz . . . zzzz.

There could be another explanation, Malcolm thought. He remembered when he was

seven and his hamster, Frodo, tunneled inside the couch. It took them three days to find him. In the meantime he'd eaten a sizable hole in the back.

That's it, Malcolm thought. A hornet had somehow gotten into his room and flown up into his mattress. He'd just crawl under and trap it in a jar. Then he could set it free outside.

He smiled at how silly he'd been. Malcolm got on his knees, leaned over, peeked under the bed and, *"Ahhhhhhh!"* A twisted face with bulbous black eyes peered out at him.

Malcolm jumped back, his heart *thump-thump-thumping*. He had to get out of there! He leaped off the bed, but a thin, hairy arm reached out and clutched his ankle. "Oh no!"

The creature shimmied out from under the bed, and that's when Malcolm saw its two noses. Well, not really noses. He recognized them as a proboscis—the feeding snout of a fly. Yes, it was a fly. A fly the size of Bigfoot! And it had a strong grip on Malcolm's leg.

Malcolm panicked. He couldn't match the Fly's strength as it dragged him closer and closer. No way was he going to let this droning bedbug beat him. The Fly had hold of one ankle, but Malcolm was in control of the other. He pivoted and – *clomp!* – he stamped down on the Fly's arm. It squealed and let go.

Malcolm wasted no time. He blasted through his bedroom door, turned into the hall, and – *wham!* – slammed right into another hideous creature!

"Watch it, you idiot!" Cocoa yelled as she slammed him against the wall.

"W-what are you doing up?" Malcolm asked, his voice still quaking.

"I couldn't sleep, Freakface. I was going into the kitchen to get a glass of milk."

Malcolm barely heard her. He kept glancing back toward his room. Was the Fly waiting? Watching? Was it behind the door? In the closet? Should he shove Cocoa in to find out?

"Now, get out of my way," Cocoa ordered. She tromped down the hall to the kitchen.

Malcolm peeked into his room but didn't see the fly. But he didn't want to take any chances either. Once Cocoa was back in bed, he slipped into the living room and slept on the couch.

Phantom of the What?

Malcolm dragged himself to the bus stop the next morning. The couch was fine for watching TV, but not for a long night of chilling nightmares.

When he'd finally gone back into his room to get dressed, he spotted a tiny housefly bumping at his bedroom window. He opened it and let the fly zoom away. Could he have heard that fly last night and dreamed about the monstrous movie version?

No. He knew what he saw. It had been just as real as Godzilla's paintball invasion and the Creature's storm drain escape.

When he reached the corner, Dandy was bent over, zipping his backpack.

"Hey," Malcolm greeted.

Dandy jolted about two feet into the air and screamed. A wad of gum shot out of his mouth and hit a telephone pole. He placed his hand over his heart and panted. "You scared the bubblegum out of me!"

"Sorry," Malcolm said. "I thought you saw me. Why are you so jumpy?"

"You'd be jumpy too if you'd seen what I saw last night."

Malcolm couldn't imagine Dandy seeing anything worse than the monster movie version of the Fly. "I had a rough night, too."

"What happened?" Dandy asked.

Malcolm shook his head. "You first."

Dandy's face scrunched up like he was scared to say. Finally, "It happened about three o'clock this morning. Some loud, creepy music woke me up. At first I was mad because I was having this great dream about winning a trip to Hollywood.

"I was in a limousine, only it wasn't really a limousine, it was more like a roller coaster. There was a movie producer sitting next to me. He had teeth so white I had to wear sunglasses. Anyway, he handed me a contract to be in his next movie. It was an action thriller with lots of explosions and car chases and—"

"Dandy!" Malcolm interrupted. "What happened after you woke up?"

"I heard strange music coming from the living room. Someone was playing my

48

mom's piano. I knew it wasn't my mom because she only plays and sings songs from the '80s."

Malcolm cringed. "Ew."

"I know," Dandy said. "She thinks she's Madonna. But this music sounded eerie, like something from a zombie movie."

"So what'd you do?" Malcolm asked.

"I slipped out of bed and tiptoed to the living room. That's when I saw this man hunched over at the piano."

"A man?"

"Yeah," Dandy said. "At first I thought it was Dad, even though he can't play anything but 'Chopsticks' and he messes that up, too. Anyway, I said, 'Dad?' But he didn't answer. He just kept playing that crazy music."

"What'd you do?" Malcolm wondered.

"I crept up behind him. I wanted to see who it was."

"Who was it?" Malcolm urged.

Dandy's eyes bulged. "At first I didn't know. The guy was wearing some kind of mask. So I snuck up closer, reached over, and plucked it off his face . . ."

"And?" Malcolm said.

Dandy looked like he might throw up. "And I had about fifteen heart attacks! His face was all twisted and gnarled and burnt, like he got too close to the barbecue grill. I couldn't believe it, Malcolm. It was the Phantom of the Opera!"

"Whoa!" Malcolm said, taking a step back. "What'd you do then?"

"I shot out of there and ran to my parents' bedroom. I tried telling my dad that the Phantom of the Opera was playing some freaky music on our piano, but he didn't believe me. Mostly because the Phantom plays the organ, not the piano. He sent me back to my room."

"Then what happened?" Malcolm asked.

"Nothing. I peeked into the living room and the Phantom was gone. Guess he

saw some of my mom's sheet music from the '80s." Then Dandy asked, "So what happened to you last night?"

Malcolm was about to tell him when—*Ow-ooooooo!*—something howled.

"What was that?" Dandy asked.

Malcolm had no idea. "I think it was just a dog."

Ow-ooooooo!

Dandy's eyes bulged again. "I've never heard a dog howl like that."

Malcolm glanced around. He had the feeling they were being watched.

Ow-ooooooo!

"It sounds like a wolf," Dandy said, shifting his backpack up like he was preparing to run.

Malcolm agreed. But that was silly. A wolf in this neighborhood? There was more concrete than grass, the trees were pruned back. And if a wolf did come around, Mr. Fletcher, the crotchety old man on the corner, would blast it away with his garden hose.

"It doesn't make sense for a wolf to be prowling around here," Malcolm said.

Dandy tilted his head. "And it doesn't make sense for the Creature from the Black Lagoon to live in a storm drain. Or Godzilla to invade a video game. Or the Phantom of the Opera to have a recital in my living room."

Ow-ooooooo!

Malcolm froze. "It's getting closer."

Dandy nodded. "I know."

"I think it's behind that house," Malcolm whispered, pointing to the house two doors down.

Ow-ooooooo!

Malcolm's heart thumped. What should they do? He was working on a plan when the school bus came grinding up the street. It stopped at the corner, and the boys nearly fell over each other getting in.

"That was close," Dandy huffed, as they took their seats.

But Malcolm didn't say a word. He couldn't speak. He just tapped Dandy on the shoulder and pointed. Peeking from behind a tree was a tall man with a wolf's face and hands.

Dandy's teeth rattled. "It—it's a werewolf," he murmured.

Malcolm shook his head. "Not just any werewolf, Dandy. It's the Wolfman."

"But . . . but . . . but," Dandy sputtered, "it's not a full moon."

"Dandy," Malcolm said, "it's not even night!"

Dandy slumped into his seat. "Why is this happening?" he wanted to know. "Why are we seeing these movie monsters?"

Malcolm gave it some thought. It had to be tied to Horrorfest. But what's the connection? Then suddenly it made sense.

"I think I know why," Malcolm told Dandy. "And after school, we're going to put a stop to it."

Monster Mash

After school, Malcolm rushed to his basement lab and packed up the two tools he used the most. His Ecto-Handheld-Automatic-Heat-Sensitive-Laser-Enhanced Specter Detector, and its companion, the ever-reliable ghost zapper.

He met Dandy on the corner, and they pedaled off toward the Bijou Theater.

"Let's go a different way," Dandy suggested. "I don't want to pass that storm drain again."

"Good thinking," Malcolm said as he cut to the right.

The old theater was dead quiet. Horrorfest was gone, and the letters on the marquee spelled one simple word: *Closed*.

"It shut down already?" Dandy said, locking his bike on the bike rack.

Malcolm locked his bike, too. "That was quick. But this could make things easier for us."

He knew the front doors would be locked, but he jiggled them anyway.

"You need a ticket to get in," a voice rattled.

"Who said that?" Dandy asked, his eyes blooming wide.

They slowly turned toward the box office window. Dandy stumbled back, knocking against Malcolm.

"Wh-wh-what?" he stuttered.

Inside the booth sat a clackety gray skeleton. He wore a small red hat and waved movie tickets up and down with his bony fingers.

Malcolm stood tall. "You don't scare us!"

"Yes, he does," Dandy said, cowering behind him.

"Come on," Malcolm told Dandy. "Let's go round back. We'll find a way in. And we won't need a ticket, Bonehead!" he spat at the skeleton.

Malcolm was right. One exit door just needed a hefty tug to pull it open. They peeked in, then entered the dark, musty theater.

The only noise inside was the *twack, twack, twack* of their sneakers stepping across the sticky floor.

"Don't they ever mop this place?" Dandy asked.

Malcolm wondered that, too. "Maybe after years of spilled sodas and greasy popcorn it's just part of the floor."

But the more they trudged, the harder it became to move.

"This is weird," Malcolm said. "It feels like we're stuck in quicksand."

Dandy nodded. "Maybe it's that cursed bubblegum again."

"Or maybe it's—" He looked down at his feet. "The Blob!"

Yikes! They were both caught in the grip of the famous globular goo.

Dandy grabbed his leg and tugged. "What are we going to do?"

Malcolm looked around for something to pull them away. All he could do was clutch the nearest chair and hang on.

"My legs are numb!" Dandy squealed. "I can't feel them! It's eaten my legs!"

Malcolm noticed his legs were ice cold, too.

Just then, an usher rushed down the aisle holding a fire extinguisher. His black suit didn't exactly match the tiny red hat tilted on his head. "Let me help."

"Thank you!" Malcolm said, wondering if the guy really could pull them loose.

"Hurry, Mister," Dandy urged. He was now waist-deep in blob.

The usher pulled the trigger on the extinguisher, blasting the Blob full force.

It recoiled, loosening its grip on the boys. Then with a frosty crackle, it turned into a giant igloo-shaped ice cube.

"Wow!" Malcolm said. "That was pretty good."

The usher patted the fire extinguisher, then gave the Blob one more quick blast. "Everyone knows that the only way to get rid of the Blob is to freeze him."

"Thanks a bunch," Malcolm said. "You saved our lives."

The usher set the fire extinguisher down, took off his hat, and straightened his suit. "Well, I couldn't let the Blob have you all to himself." He turned and smiled at the boys, flashing fangs as long as his slender fingers. *Hssssssssss.*

Dandy clawed into Malcolm's shirt. "You're a vampire!"

The vampire bowed. "You can call me Count Dracula."

Oh no! Now they were in even bigger trouble. *Think! Think!* Malcolm thought. There had to be some way out of this. He didn't want to end up as Dracula's afternoon tea.

Dandy quivered. "M-M-Malcolm, do we have any garlic?"

"No," Malcolm said. "But we have this." He reached down, snatched up the fire extinguisher, and whacked Dracula across the knee.

"Ow!" the Count yelped, hopping on one foot.

"Run for the door!" Malcolm shouted. He and Dandy shot away, racing around the Blob and across the icky floor.

But Dracula was quick. He morphed into a bat and winged his way toward them, squeaking, *Eek–eek–eek*.

"Run, Dandy, run!" Malcolm urged.

The bat swooped and dived, aiming for their necks. *Eek–eek–eek*.

They covered their heads, swatting when it came close.

Eek–eek–eek.

"He's going to get me," Dandy cried. "He's going to drink my blood."

"No, he's not," Malcolm said.

Then, just as the vampire circled and dove, Malcolm kicked open the door and ducked. The bat flew over his head right out into the afternoon sun.

Eek–eek–eek? He lit up like a sparkler, then – *pfft* – fizzled out.

Malcolm grinned. "The Blob doesn't like cold, and Dracula doesn't like daylight."

Dandy let out a huffy sigh. "Right. Now can we get this over with?"

"Yep." Malcolm set his backpack down and pulled out his ghost detector. He powered it on and aimed it at the projection booth window. Behind the glass sat a

mousy little ghost wearing a yellow-checkered shirt and wire spectacles. He flipped a switch on the projector and an old black-and-white film flickered onto the screen.

"What's playing?" Dandy asked.

"Who cares," Malcolm answered. "Let's hurry before he sends another monster after us."

They darted up the aisle to the balcony. It was blocked off by a faded velvet rope. Malcolm pointed to a small door at the top. "He's in there."

They dipped under the rope, but something didn't feel right. That's when the rope popped loose, coiled around them, and squeeeeeeeezed.

Dandy wiggled and squirmed. "What's going on?"

"I don't know," Malcolm answered. That's when he noticed that the velvety rope was turning a coarse green and sprouting leaves. "It feels like we're wrapped in a jungle vine."

"What monster movie takes place in a jungle?" Dandy asked.

Malcolm didn't need to answer. On the other side of the balcony rose a black hairy face with two ape eyes and flaring nostrils.

Dandy's eyes bugged. "It's King Kong!"

The giant gorilla snorted a breath of stinky snot at them.

"Ew! That's grosser than the theater floor," Dandy said, his face glistening.

King Kong leaned in closer. He tilted his head left and right with a curious look

on his face. Then he reached a giant hairy
paw over the railing and grabbed Dandy.

"Noooooo!" Dandy cried as the huge
ape plucked him free of the vine.

That caused the vine to sag just enough
for Malcolm to kick his way free.

"Malcolm, help!"

"I'll save you, Dandy!" Malcolm grabbed his gear and ran up toward the projection booth.

"Malcolm! You're going the wrong way. Can't you see? I'm over here."

King Kong pinched Dandy's collar and dangled him high. Then with his other hand, he thumped at Dandy's feet to make him dance.

"Malcolm! Do something. I don't like being King Kong's action figure!"

Malcolm was already inside the projection booth, his zapper aimed at the scrawny ghost. "Turn off that machine!" He could see then that the main feature was indeed *King Kong*.

"Just go ahead and zap me," the gaunt little ghost said. "I don't care. I have nothing to live for."

Huh? "Uh . . . you're not living," Malcolm said. "You're a ghost."

"Whatever," the ghost said, dismissing Malcolm with a wave.

"Let my friend go!" Malcolm ordered. Through the projection window, he could see King Kong sniffing Dandy up and down. Dandy was pummeling Kong's nose, but it didn't seem to matter.

The ghostly man huffed. "Well, are you going to zap me or not?"

"Not," Malcolm said. "Not until you tell me why you sent a pack of movie monsters after us."

"Not just movie monsters. *Classic* movie monsters."

"Who are you?" Malcolm asked.

"Oh, how rude of me. My name is Cal Trantham. I'm the projectionist here. I have been for half a century."

"I'm pretty sure you're not the projectionist anymore." Malcolm snuck a peek through the window. King Kong now had Dandy dangling by one foot.

"I opened this theater," Cal said. "I was the very first projectionist. And now they're shutting it down. Soon it will become a flea market, or it may just sit and rot. And when it goes, my beloved movie creatures will go with it. They'll vanish. No one will see them again."

"I'm pretty sure everyone will see them again," Malcolm said. "Anytime they want."

"That's just not possible," Cal argued.

"Of course it is," Malcolm said. "Haven't you heard of DVDs?"

"Isn't that some type of long underwear?" Cal asked.

"No," Malcolm said. "It's a disc that has a movie on it. You play it in a DVD player."

Cal just stared at him. He clearly had no clue what Malcolm was talking about.

"Trust me," Malcolm said. "People can watch movies in their homes now. And plenty of people watch these old horror films. Horrorfests are fun, but we don't need them anymore."

Malcolm heard laughter. Dandy was still dangling, but now King Kong was tickling his ribs.

"So let's just turn off this machine," Malcolm said, stepping over to the projector.

"No," Cal argued, leaping out of his seat. He spun the projector toward

Malcolm, blinding him with the bright bulb. "Never!"

"Yes," Malcolm said, pushing the projector away.

"No," Cal insisted, turning the projector back on Malcolm.

"Yes," Malcolm demanded.

"No!" Cal shouted.

"Yes!" Malcolm placed the ghost zapper right in front of Cal's nose and pressed the trigger. Cal crossed his eyes, looked down at his feet, then bubbled to the floor.

Malcolm clicked off the projector, causing King Kong to vanish. And with an *"Aiii-ooh!"* Dandy fell to the floor.

Oh no! Malcolm tore out of the booth and down the stairs. "Dandy!" he yelled, hoping his friend hadn't broken his neck.

Dandy sat in the middle of the aisle, covered in Kong spit. He crept to his feet. "I feel like a wet puppet."

"Let's go," Malcolm said. "It's over."

Dandy looked at the seat of his pants. He had four kernels of popcorn, a wad of bubblegum, and a chocolate candy wrapper stuck to his bottom.

"It's never over," he said.

Face-Frenemies

Malcolm made it home in time for dinner. "I'm here," he called. "Sorry I'm late."

Everyone sat quietly as Mom served up the salad and lasagna. Even Cocoa was silent. *Cocoa's not yakking? Really? This must be bad.*

"Is something wrong?" Malcolm asked, taking his spot at the table.

Grandma Eunice looked at him, sour faced. "You betcha," she said, practically growling the words. "Your mother made me take down my Face-Friends page."

Cocoa giggled a little. But Grandma gave her the stink eye and she hushed.

Malcolm gulped. This had to be bad. "No more Face-Friends Fogies?"

"You miss all the good stuff," Cocoa said, a little giggly again.

Dad sat behind a newspaper, pretending to read. Malcolm knew family meals were important, so if Dad was hiding, it had to be really bad.

"I didn't do anything wrong!" Grandma barked, defending herself. "I was just catching up with an old friend."

That's when Malcolm noticed Grandma's mouth looked shriveled and

shrunk, like she'd bitten into a lemon. Her dentures were gone! Now he was oozing with curiosity.

"Which friend?" he urged.

Grandma sliced into her lasagna and stared at it on the end of her fork. Malcolm wondered how long it would take her to chew once it was in her mouth. She grunted and set the fork down. "I friended my old high school boyfriend, Lester Funderburk."

Cocoa giggled again. This time Mom directed the stink eye at her.

Grandma continued, "Lester and I were just catching up, talking about the good old days."

"It was nice to be in touch again," Grandma continued. "But it turned out he was dating a floozy at his nursing home. She found out and got angry."

"Angry?" Mom spat.

"Okay," Grandma surrendered. "She was madder than a bee-stung billy goat. She came over here and threatened me. I told her that Lester was my boyfriend, but she wouldn't have any of that. She tried to slug me with her purse."

"What'd you do?" Malcolm asked.

"I backed up and wheeled away! Then she started chasing me. I managed to stay ahead of her for a while."

Dad grunted and turned the page of his newspaper.

"But how?" Malcolm wondered. "Couldn't she outrun your wheelchair?"

"Not with that clunky old walker of hers!"

"And Cocoa didn't help you?" Malcolm asked.

Grandma waved her off. "Naw, she was too busy rolling around on the floor laughing. I was winning that race. But then she cheated. Once I made it to the kitchen, she ran around the other way. Stopped me head on.

"I tried to back up, but she came at me with that monster purse. I reached over and grabbed the canister of flour and flung it all over her. A direct hit! She was covered in it. White as a ghost."

Malcolm grinned at that. Most of the ghosts he'd met weren't exactly white, just see-through.

"But she still got the best of me," Grandma said. "That crazy old biddy lunged over her walker, snatched my teeth right out of my mouth, dropped them in her purse, and hobbled away. I tried to chase her down, but she hurried off like a

jackrabbit. So now she has Lester and my choppers."

Grandma sighed. "That's why I had to take down my Face-Friends page. Too much drama." She finally stuffed one of the long noodles in her mouth and gummed it a little.

"That's okay, Grandma," Malcolm said. "I can ride over to that nursing home tomorrow and get your dentures back."

"You'd do that?" Grandma asked.

"Sure," he said.

Mom glared at her. "And no more Face-Friends."

"No more Face-Friends," Grandma agreed. She leaned toward Malcolm and whispered, "I found a new site. Cyber-Pals."

Oh no!

TOOLS OF THE TRADE: FIVE TOOLS FOR THE GHOST HUNTER ON THE GO

From Ghost Detectors Malcolm and Dandy

Sometimes, ghost detectors have to use the things around them to fight a ghost. Always be aware of your surroundings and use them to your advantage!

1. Fire extinguishers are useful for beating the Blob.

2. Watch for exits to send vampires out into the sun.

3. Keep a gorilla handy to pluck you out of vines that grow on their own.

4. Have a stash of acrobatic tricks up your sleeve to entertain the gorilla in number 3.

5. Always take along your best friend, it's the best tool you've got! He or she can distract a monster, zap a ghost, and get you home in time for dinner.